D0497899

A Novel in Doodles

LOS GATOS PUBLIC LIBRARY
LOS GATOS, CALIFORNIA

Doodlebug

A Novel in Doodles

by

Karen Romano Young

FEIWEL AND FRIENDS
NEW YORK

A FEIWEL AND FRIENDS BOOK
An Imprint of Macmillan

DOODLEBUG. Copyright © 2010 by Karen Romano Young. All rights reserved.
Distributed in Canada by H.B. Fenn and Company Ltd. Printed in November 2010
in the United States of America by R. R. Donnelley & Sons Company, Crawfordsville, Indiana.
For information, address Feiwel and Friends, 175 Fifth Avenue, New York, NY 10010.

Library of Congress Cataloging-in-Publication Data Available

ISBN: 978-0-312-56156-7

Book design by Kathleen Breitenfeld

Feiwel and Friends logo designed by Filomena Tuosto

First Edition: 2010

10 9 8 7 6 5 4 3

www.feiwelandfriends.com

For **Emily**, with love from Schmuel.

Thank you, !!!

Thank you, J. Alison James and the MARCH MADNESS authors.

Thank you, Bill, Staci, and **SVEN**.

Thank you, NOON, for the buck teeth.

A Novel in Doodles

(The End.)

1. L.A.

DOODLEBUG

oreen   ussery

NO!

IT started when my parents went and decided to move.

Me and my sister, Momo, didn't get to say anything about it. We just had to get in the car and go. Our dad is a graphic designer and he got a new job, so that was that. No discussion...

LA

What do you like best, Momo? La La La or sssff?

FROM →

I like L.A. best!

TO →

SF

SF.
L.A.
CALIFORNIA

CUT IT OUT, DODO!

as if I listened!

We got stuff to use on the LONG ride for entertainment! Not so thrilling.

The blank book was supposed to be for the license plate game or lists of places to visit or hangman.

But I started drawing and didn't stop. I didn't do anything but draw THE WHOLE WAY.

Mom, Dodo put all her stickers on the headrest.

trip / trap / wrap / crap / clap / flap / flop

Mom thinks a word ladder would be good entertainment.

NOT ME

There was only one word that I thought was interesting the whole trip.

Ojai →

"O. J.," read Momo. But Mom said, "It's pronounced, 'Oh, hi.'"

MOMO got all excited. "I've never been to a place named with a name like that!" she said. I wanted to slow down getting to S.F., so I asked, "The J is like in Spanish, right?" My MOM is a writer, and she's in ♡ with words.

BLINK BLINK FLASH FLASH

California GO 4 IT

So we hung a Ralph and stopped in Ojai for lunch. Here is what happened in Ojai:

1. We bought drinks. Dad (real name Warren) likes the designs on Sobe bottles. Mom (real name Jolene) burps her way (politely) through Diet Coke. Momo collects Snapple lids for the factoids printed there. I like Fusion, but they didn't have it in Ojai. I was in the mood to draw the bottle but I don't care," I said.

2. I didn't want to talk. So I got my blank book out of the car and tried drawing this cool tower.

no. <u>lopsided.</u>

no. <u>flat.</u>

no. <u>CRIPES!</u>

for the first time I started to cry.

DAD came over and looked at my paper. I yelled like a freak.

DON'T LOOK! No No No No No No No

"**DODO**," he said. "Just keep drawing."

Here, Dad.

I finally finished. →

...ey had let us stay ...Ojai until I got ...he picture of the ...ost office tower to ...ook more or less O.K. I didn't think you ...ere ever going to ...top drawing," said

Momo. I said, ...aybe I <u>won't</u> stop!"

ZZZZZzzz:

Momo started snoring right away.

"How about you?" Mom asked me.

"Are you going to faire dodo?"

♪♫♪ fais dodo ♪♫♪ is a song.

I'm not sleeping, hahaha.

I'm not French, either!

My mom loves words in any language.

She used to sing to me,

"fais dodo, ma petite cherie."

It means "make sleep, my little dear." (Not cherry)

BUT I NEVER DID.

Hahaha. My name is Doreen. But Dodo stuck

Momo's name means "peach" in Japanese.

We're not Japanese, either.

Mom found the name in a book called Umbrella.

The little girl in Umbrella is named Momo.

I said,

Why didn't you name her Umbrella?

Because my Mom just likes words, get it?
(Momo's real name is Maureen.)

Warren (39) (DAD)   Jolene (MOM) (41)

Doreen (12) (DODO)   Maureen (MOMO) (10½)

$= 4$ All the people I know in all San Francisco.

age total: 102½

We drove another hundred miles, and Momo made ZZZZs. I drew some more. I was having a lot of **DARK** thoughts about what was at the other end of this road.

RATS!!!!!!

"Are we going to stop anywhere else?" I asked.

"How about that almond stand?" said Dad.

The ☀ was warm like the stickers on the headrest, and Momo stayed asleep as we bought almonds.

"You know, Dodo," said Mom. "In a new school you can be a whole new person. You can be ANYONE YOU WANT."

NUTS!!!!!

I liked my old school. I knew who everybody was. I knew where everything was. I didn't have to be a whole new person. I could be myself. I want to go HOME.

"Fine then!!!" I said.

"From now on, my name is...

⟶

Doodlebug

Mom was driving, so I handed my book to Dad.

"Doodlebug," he read. He showed the page to Mom. "ART IS POWER," he said.

Mom said, "THE PEN IS MIGHTIER THAN THE SWORD." Then she said, "Shut up please, everyone. This road is getting very curly."

Dad gave me back my book. He said, "ROCK ON, DODO." I said, "Doodlebug!" And I added, "I rule!"

"You DROOL," said momo

FACT #1: making all those dots, I felt the →POWER←

FACT #2: Mom did say curly, not curvy.

AND IT WAS GETTING cliffy.

"Do you want me to drive?" asked Dad sweetly.

"NO!" said Mom unsweetly

"You don't have to be such a hero," said Dad.

BUT even after we stopped at a fruit stand, she drove.

"We've got to face our fears," said MOM

Momo ate a peach. I drew strawberries. Dad worried.

← Pacific Ocean
← beach
← really high cliff!!
← small strip of grass
← balcony with chairs
← suitcases and backpacks
← Mom and Dad (FREAKING OUT)
← their light, still on
← our light, off
← I'm supposed to sleep here.
← Momo makes dodo.
← Sink, potty
← bathtub, where Dodo makes doodles....

HOTEL
..CANCY

I have occasionally sleepwalked. ZZZZz...

"She can't sleepwalk over the cliff with all those bags blocking the door."

"She won't even come out of the john, she's so nervous."

"Nervous about MOVING, not sleepwalking! But she's in there DRAWING, not peeing!"

"She's wigging out. Did you see all those strawberries? She's obsessive! Oh, I hope this school is better...."

"She's not still drawing strawberries. She's fine. It's a creative outlet. You've got the JITTERS."

"Wouldn't you? Shouldn't I? No job, tiny apartment... And tomorrow it all starts, after a hundred more miles of CLIFFS!!"

I'm not listening. I'm not listening. I'm drawing something just for Mom... for Mom, who's so scared of CLIFFS....

* white knuckles

Mom survived.

"Did my funeral help?"

"What is your PROBLEM?" asked Momo.

"It was the WORST-CASE SCENARIO," said Dad.

"And that means what?"

What's the worst that could HAPPEN? (said Dad.)   24 miles

CALIFORNIA POPPIES

"The worst that could happen," said Momo softly, "is if Dodo got expelled from school again."

"That situation is under control," said Mom firmly.

"It wasn't your fault anyway," murmured Dad.

"YES, IT WAS!" I exclaimed. "IT WAS ONLY MY FAULT!"

What I did:

DUH

I decided that if I "got" to take Ritalin, everyone else should share the privilege. So I passed out my whole prescription to my class, and gave them each an invoice for 25¢ a pill. I made $11.50. Ricky Munson told. I was a moron.

THEN   THEY   ALL   HATED   ME

S.F.???

S.F.?

S.F....

S.F.!!!

(Getting There.)

2. S.F.

THE OCEAN LOOKS DIFFERENT NEAR SAN FRANCISCO

Everything Happens at the Right Time

Mom has sayings.
She says this one now, brightly: (Shut up shut up Shut up!

[Dodo] [did] [what] [she] [thought] [she] [needed] [to] [d

Dad makes statements.
Sometimes I wonder if he mixes up his words like magnetic poems.

(Shut shut shut up up up!)

Then he added, "When you see a [windmill] we'll be almost

There."

We saw it.
I reached out and picked up
Momo's hand. Her hand was
sweating. My heart was beating.

Momo whispered,

"It's going to be all right."

"Shut up!!!"

THE HOUSE

Then we got there.
IS TALL AND GREEN.
IT HAS A PINE TREE TH
IS TALL AND GREEN
AND WHEN WE FIRST
GOT THERE, I SAW A
BLACK CAT IN THE
TOP LEFT WINDOW:
OUR WINDOW.

3 months!

JANUARY · FEBRUARY · MARCH

That is how long we have in this apartment.

It is a sublet. It's Staci's apartment. Staci is Dad's college friend who is in Japan. The only thing I knew about Staci before now is a picture she made in illustration class for an assignment. They had to illustrate an everyday saying. Staci did "buck teeth" and it looked like this:

They are antlers growing out of crooked teeth.

Dad had hung it on his office wall in L.A. Where was it now?

He says it was the beginning of Staci's dental art. Momo, who has braces, thought he meant those colored thingers you can get on your braces for your color-coordinated outfit. But Dad picked up a DVD and said, "This is her." Staci is an animator now. She made:

Mouth the Almighty

Mouth the Almighty was a superhero set of choppers with feet, arms, eyes, and a gum-pink cape. On the back of the DVD it said,

Her bite is worse than her bark.

☺ "Ouch," said Dad. "That's Staci for ya."

STACI'S LIVING ROOM WINDOW LOOKED OUT INTO THE BIG TREE. MOMO AND I WERE GOING TO SLEEP ON THE DAYBED HERE THAT HAD A QUILT WITH THE PATTERN OF "FLYING GEESE." I KNOW FROM A REPORT I DID: SLAVES HUNG THIS QUILT WHEN IT WAS TIME TO RUN AWAY. UNDER THE BED WE FOUND SVEN. HISS!!

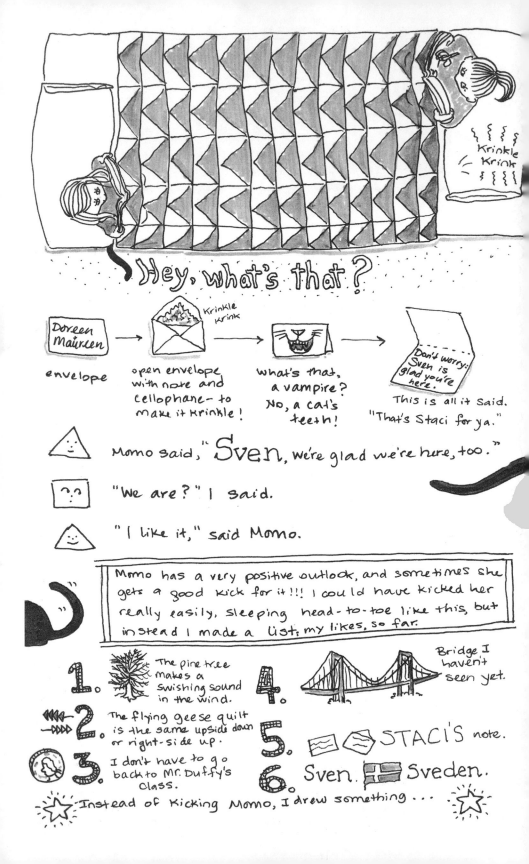

SOME THOUGHTS ON MR. DUFFY

He said he was just trying to keep one student from disrupting twenty-one others but

Wassamatta, Dodo, you can't faire DODO?

I was just doodling, Dad.

I wanted to ask you something, Dodo. What's up with all the drawing?

I don't know.

Staci says when she draws, she finds her sense of humor.

Isn't she funny anyway?

What I mean is, what are you finding?

I don't know. I just like it.

Try harder, Dodo. What do you think about?

Nothing.

You just want to draw.

I'm the Doodlebug.

Mr. Duffy didn't understand very much.

HE LOOKED!!

I AM NOT THERE ANYMORE SO HAHAHA

In the morning, we went and saw the city of San Francisco. It is SPECTACULAR, which Momo says means you ought to have SPECIAL SUNGLASSES to look at it.

We walked up this hill so high, I nearly died and then later we came down it in a cable car and nearly died in a whole other way! Death from exhaustion, then from BIG THRILLS. On the way home, I slipped back and walked with just Dad. "I'm going to be good at school," I said. He said, "I'm going to be good at work." I said, "But you were never bad." He said, "You were never bad either."

My Secret Weapon:

STUPID OLD NEW SCHOOL STARTS

visibles:

~~invisables:~~
invisibles: *

Sweater
(It's cold here.)

oh, you know.

Skirt
(I'm trying to
make a good
impression.)

what would really
be embarrassing
would be NOT
wearing them.

bally socks

penny for luck

Vanny vans

Band·Aid in
case of unluck
(blister)

* so secret, I forgot how to spell it,
but just for a second

SUNDAY

I...DON'T...LIKE...SUNDAY...BECAUSE...TOMORROW...IS......

monday.

THIS IS OUR SCHOOL→

MIDDLE SCHOOL

MOMO THINKS ←IT'S COOL

It has columns but they are not Doric columns, which might be a good omen!

It looks like a wedding cake or a mission or a museum or a library!

7th grade

They're Corinthian columns, all carved and pretty.

Don't the trees remind you of Mom's curly hair?

5th grade

Our old school was a little private school.

This school is a big public school. Eek!

A Venn diagram:

Dad's opinions:

"You won't be just stuck in one classroom!"

"You might hear some more swearing."

"Junior high is cruelty on a cracker."

Have some cheese with that.

Shared opinions:

You'll be able to move around more.

You won't be the only loon in the lake.

Good luck. You'll need it!

Mom's opinions:

"You'll have a different teacher for every class!"

"You'll be with a more diverse group."

"They oughta build a moat around 7th grade."

Jump on in!

FIRST DAY PRECAUTIONS:

 Take $ for lunch until you figure out what people do.

Touch Sven's tail for good luck.
(He's still under the bed, dreaming of Sveden.)

 Take Doodlebook to help you remember who you are.

 Take turned-off cellphone. Get ~~told to give it~~ to Momo to hold just in case you're going to get nervous and use bad judgment and call someone. Take it back from Momo the second you're inside the school door.

WOMEN Notice where the loo-loo is just in case you have to barf, which seems likely. (In our old school, it said GIRLS.)

 Study the EMERGENCY Building EXIT sign. This is always a good idea, even better when you're scared to look at all the other MIDDLE SCHOOL STUDENTS entering. (Basically, the sign says if something catches up or blows fire * turn around and leave the building. DUH.)

 SO I'M A LITTLE NERVOUS. SUE ME!)))*

* Yes, I wrote it inside out. I like it that way!

my Vans were plain white but I made them plaid with Sharpies, just last night.

her actual socks

She walks MILES!

Ms. Wu wears KEDS so she can cover the school.

Here are the feet of the principal, Ms. Wu, taking my feet to my new homeroom. Bye, Momo.

Everybody, this is Doreen Bussey.

Ms. Keller

Ms. Keller was as short as one of the kids and shorter than lots of them. She was about the same size as Momo. (We are tall people.) And Momo is 10½! Also, (MS.K.) she was very considerate.

Doreen, do you go by a nickname?

And it just came out. Yes, it just came out, as if I had thought about that idea of being a new person at a new school.

"YES," I said. "I'm called the

DOODLEBUG"

Jordan Jamirez

A beautiful boy with sticking-up hair asked the most amazing question: "Is your nickname

DOodle BUg because your name is
DOreen BUssey?"

" my face nearly fell off because
oops! I HADN'T EVEN THOUGHT
OF THAT!!

But I just said, "Only partly." BIG LIE!!

"It's really because I'm an ARTIST.

BIG MISTAKE. Because now I have to
BE ONE.

BUSSEY, DOREEN D. 7K KELLER

	1	2	3	4	5	6	7
M	SPAN 112	SCI 345	SOC ST 218	PE / LUNCH / SHOP	LANG ART 313	ART 016	MATH 201
T				LUNCH / HOME ARTS		CHORUS 011	
W				LUNCH / SHOP		STUDY	
T				LUNCH /		CHORUS 011	
F				PE / LUNCH		ART 016	

"O.K., **7K**,ᴰᴰ" said Ms. Keller, picking up this schedule thingy of mine, "**Who's got SPANISH** in 112 with the **Doodlebug**?"

An Indian girl (Asian Indian) with **LONG BLACK BRAIDS** came over to me.

RRIIING! It is the old-school (ha ha ha) kind of bell, where you can see the ringer ringing.

"¡HOLA!" she said.

I followed the girl into the hall full of 1,000,000 (That's a million, if you can't count 0000000s) people.

"Hey, what kind of an artist are you, Doodlebug?" she asked. I said, "Well, I'm a doodler."

"**Pen and Ink?**" she asked. "Is that your medium?"

I had never thought about it before. I didn't want to say, my WHAT? I said, "Yes, and my small and **large**."

"Ha ha ha ha ha!" she laughed a **large laugh**.

"I myself work in paper."

Español was only two doors down the hall.

110 Ms. Keller | 111 Ms. Hermés | 112 Sr. Rámos

The teacher wasn't even there yet so we sat down and the girl pulled a little folded-up paper out of her backpack. She turned a corner of it up and asked,

"Can you draw something RED, just in this triangle?" "What RED?" I said. "ANYTHING!" "Cherries?" "Yeah!" I could tell there was some SPEED involved here. Quickly, I drew cherries, then an orange, a lemon,

beans, a blueberry, a bottle of ink, a sheet of paper,

and a pig. Just the head. There wasn't time for

"¡ muchas grácias !"

my new amiga said.

She stood the folded-up paper on her desk.
Turns out, it was her homework.

7Q	Pinho, Marco	✓	✓-	✓
7K	Kaur, Elizabeth	✓	✓	✓+
7E	Soldano, Sarah	✓+	✓+	✓+
7B	Furniss, Richard	✓	✓	✓
7K	Bussey, Doreen	—	—	—

The assignment (over Christmas vacation, of course) was to come up with a creative way to test people on Spanish vocabulary.

"What IS that thing?" 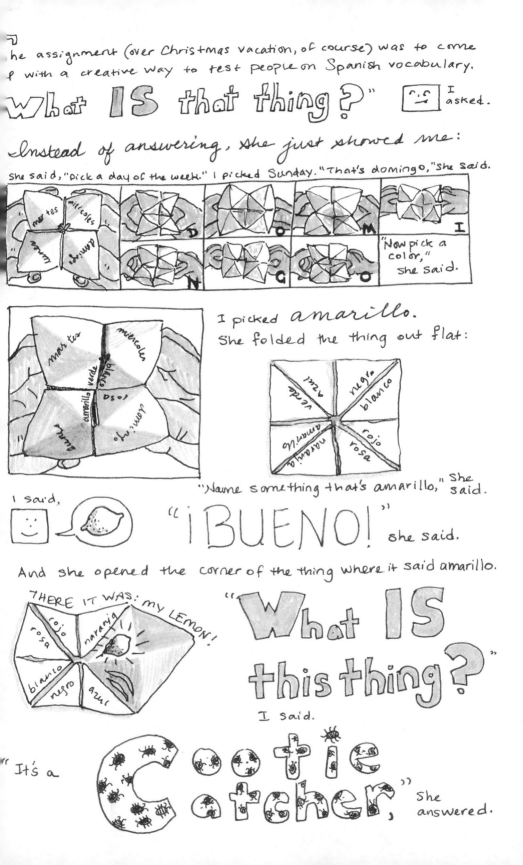 I asked.

Instead of answering, she just showed me:

She said, "pick a day of the week." I picked Sunday. "That's domingo," she said.

I picked amarillo.
She folded the thing out flat:

"Name something that's amarillo," she said.

I said, "¡BUENO!" she said.

And she opened the corner of the thing where it said amarillo.

THERE IT WAS: my LEMON! "What IS this thing?" I said.

"It's a Cootie Catcher," she answered.

The class was going on so I wrote Elizabeth Kaur a n—

really the

After class, she grabbed m[y] elbow. "Does that say I REALLY DIG THE COOTIE CATCHER?"

Yeah I said. Elizabeth said, "You really are a DOODLEBUG."

So I said, You should rename yourself COOTIE CATCHER.

"But your name's Doreen Bussey, so it's like DOodle BUg," she said. She was walking me upstairs to my science class, just to be nice. She was nice. It was all right that she had gotten me to draw on her Spanish homework. Señor Ramos had even liked the Cootie Catcher and told us how to say the things I had drawn in Spanish.

cerezas   anaranjado   limón   habas   arándano   cerdo   papel   tinta

I thought about it all through science, social studies, and the walk to PE, where Elizabeth was in my class again. It helped me not to fidget, especially in social studies, my most B O R I N G subject always.

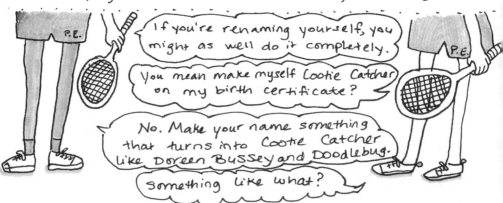

If you're renaming yourself, you might as well do it completely.

You mean make myself Cootie Catcher on my birth certificate?

No. Make your name something that turns into Cootie Catcher like Doreen Bussey and Doodlebug.

Something like what?

Colleen*Callahan *

??? I know it sounds a little Irish or something, but...

Irish! But she's

Cootie Catcher has a mean backhand. She bounced her ball right off Marco Wong's prickly head and made him stop what he was saying.

WAP!

Did you say 'BUTT CHEEKS'? I asked.

"DOOReen, COLLeen," said Marco.

Cootie Catcher said, "MARCO"...

So naturally, I answered, "POLO."

Marco went, ...grumble grumble grumble grumble...

...assamatta, boy?" I said. "You got rocks in your mouth?"

HE said, "AT HOME, I HAVE 64 prismacolor PENS."

(I bet he had at least 8 greens in that bunch, the color(s) I could have turned with pure JEALOUSY.)

Cootie Catcher said, "We all know they're your dad's, Marco."

AND MARCO said:

[4.] Monday DRAGS ON

"You should call me MAGIC MARCO."

Cootie Catcher SNORTED. "Just because your dad's an illustrator, you don't have to think you're such an ARTIST."

"Just because you know ORIGAMI doesn't mean you're such an artist either, ELIZABETH."

I felt like I had the POWER.

o o o (Peace to all people) I thought. Out loud, I said,

my mother says everyone is an artist.

Cootie Catcher said, "I HAVE MY DOUBTS ABOUT THAT."

She could be a little mean. Were they enemies? I needed help in this school. I made a decision.

I just didn't say anything else.

If they wondered what I thought (not just my mother), I was giving no more inf

I was like the Sphinx, this big statue tha is half lion, half man, in Egypt. People ask it questions, but it doesn't answer, so they have to figure it out themselves

WELL

There are not this many pyramids there, but I just like them!

I was also like Sven, keeping his thoughts to himself under the bed. In Staci's apartment, was Mom trying to find a job?

In art class, there was that triangle face again

NO. NOT MO- Me

STOOLS RULE

1. You sit up higher.
2. You sit up straighter.
3. You can turn around without scraping the floor.
4. You can wrap your feet around the legs.

AND ART HAS STOOLS!!

Plus, you can stand up to work anyway. I never get in trouble, in ART.

"How come you don't have your PRISMACOLORS?" I asked. "Where are your pens, Magic Marco?"

"My dad's worried something will happen to them at school." Magic Marco looked a little suspicious. "What about you?"

I SHOWED HIM THE TOOLS OF MY TRADE: Pilot P-700 fine point

PILOT

FABER-CASTELL

Faber-Castell Pitt artist pen brush-point in light grey

"I WORK IN BLACK + WHITE."

I didn't want him to think I cared too much about all those Prismacolors. I didn't have a single one to my name, but Dad used to have the use of them at his old work, so their wondrousness is known to me. But I don't have one, so I can't draw one here and anyway, here came the art teacher,

MR. HILL, who looked like black ALBERT EINSTEIN.

BOMBS AWAY!

Doodlebug? Well, let's see what you can do with CLAY.

WOOSH!

WHACK!

SPLAT!

He threw clay and yelled!!!

The Stages of CLAY

First, it is underwater in a river or lake, so it has water in it. It needs to stay wet.

So you dig out a lump and dry it with rags.

Use a wire to cut some off.

There will be air bubbles inside.

Now WEDGE it! Throw it down HARD! over and over!

If you don't wedge clay enough, then what you make will have air in it, and it will blow up or crack in the kiln. SO WEDGE IT!!

WWAM!

DO WE HAVE TO YELL WHEN WE'RE WEDGING CLAY?

They put me down in the basement because I am a troll and nobody cares if we make noise here.

FAIR ENOUGH!

I became a wedging champion at that moment.

BIM!

Whack!

Mr. Hill says loudly, "while you're wedging, think about what you'd like to make with your clay." wedge wedge wedge wedge wedge wedge wedge wedge wedge

I'm going to make a model Sven. It can keep him company under the bed or remind Staci what he looks like on days when he won't come out.

IN CHINATOWN, there are statues of waving cats. I think I'll make a "beckoning cat" to wave to Sven. Maybe he'll realize the world can be an okay place.

That afternoon,

I told him about it as I lay next to him under the bed. It was what happened the last period that had sent me there. COULD BE BAD.

Sven understands WORST-CASE SCENARIO thinking. That's why he stays under the bed. What he thinks might happen if he came out is worse than how it feels hiding under the bed. I understand, Sven.

YOU CAN TRUST ME, SVENNY.

We try thinking positively.........

It's a pretty school and I get to change classes.

It's safe here in the dark.

I made two friends who think it's cool to draw and they even called me Doodlebug.

Dodo's not trying to make me come out.

Spanish is good because you get to talk a lot.

I'm warm.

You can ask questions a lot in science and the teacher doesn't get mad.

I'm not hungry yet.

Art... Gym... Lunch: Fine!

The bed has me covered.

But then the worries return......

Social Studies... English... Math: Those are the kind of classes where I can't sit still.

Soon it will be night and the mice will come into the apartment.

I'll go to the lav too much or talk out or bother someone. I'll have to...

They'll eat my leftover food and I'll have to...

YOW!

MEOW!

It took **4** Band-Aids to patch me up.

"Thanks, Mo," I said sadly.

"What did you DO to him, anyway?"

(ME do to HIM*??)

* Sven, of course. Evil Sven.

"All I did was TOUCH him.

dumbcatrottencatmeancatstupidcatdidn'the knowI wanted to love him?!

Momo wouldn't let it go. She never lets things go. She said again

"What happened?"

"He was scared," I said. "I wanted to make him feel better. So, I tried petting him. I guess some cats don't like petting.

Poor baby! We looked up and Mom was in the doorway. She had on her job interview clothes, which she had bought in L.A. when we decided to move here. Paper doll Mom.

mousse-y, organized hair...

light gray suit with nautical flair...

buttoned-up shirt (red + white)...

control-top panty hose...

...and worst of all, real shoes,

at least they're red.

"Tell me all about your day," said Mom in a way we knew meant not to ask about hers.

"Sven ATTACKED DODO," said.

"I was just trying to pet him."

"It's going to take PATIENCE, Dodo."
→→→→→→→

Everything takes PATIENCE!!!

☹ I 😠 yelled 😵 impatiently. ☹ "And I don't HAVE any!!"

OMO was using up all the BAND-AIDS sticking them on herself.

She said, "ODO, I think you had patience right up to the moment you tried touching Sven."

☹ I said, "If you don't try, how will you ever know?"

"☺" Mom shook her head, thinking to herself, and said, "Exactly right." Then she added, "Tell me more."

(TELL ME MORE. That's what she always says when we come home from school to tell her stuff. But it feels like a million years since I heard her say it -- way back in December, before I got expelled but after the Ritalin started but before I started just pretending to take it, after I found it made me feel like the tortoise in the story of The Tortoise and the Hare. SLOW AND STEADY is NOT how I want to run the race.)

😐 "My math teacher already HATES me!"

I announced horribly. "He ripped my notes right out of my binder and gave me a great big check minus in front of the whole class and said, 'NOTES ARE GRADED!' He said, 'And NO DOODLING!'"

Doreen "Doodlebug" Bussey
Mr. Juarez, period 7

See me!

$x = 2$

$x = -2$
$y = -2$

"THEN, YOU CAN'T DOODLE."

I will die if I cannot doodle. It's just that simple. Mr. Juarez going to wreck my whole plan of survival at this cool school where I already have two nice friends and where I know new words in Spanish and where you can play tennis and wedge clay with a crazy Albert Einstein genius teacher (well, I mean I don't play tennis with Mr. Hill but it might be jolly).

Your plan of survival at your new school is to doodle?

"OBVIOUSLY!" I said.

momo said, "But you'll get in trouble." "OBVIOUSLY!" I said again.

But WHY? "Because I found out =

Things are better when I draw."

It sounded like one of Mom's sayings that sound good, but I wasn't exactly sure what it meant.

Maybe, or maybe not, Mom knew how I felt. She said,

Number 1: I believe it. I'd go cuckoo if I couldn't write.

Number 2: But you are going to have to prove it to your school by doing really really well.

Number 3: Or you are going to have to consider trying the Ritalin again.

momo said, **Number 4:** Doodle Power!!!

But leave Sven in peace. "I will," I said.

Then Mom said, "How was your day, Momo?"

I felt very small, then. Because I hadn't even asked.

"Fine," said Momo. Well, that's what she always says. But...

I said, "But?" It was her eyes. She was worrying.

"What?" Momo asked me. I shrugged my shoulders.
I waited. I knew what I knew.
Then she said, "There's a choir at our new school.
You have to try out. I never tried out for anything
before. And I really want to get in it. There aren't even
any spaces because it's the middle of the year. I probably
won't be able to do it and then you can't try again until
September and maybe we won't even be here then, you
know, because it might not work out for everybody else.
But they do a giant concert in that beautiful
CATHEDRAL and they perform at the Moscone Center and—"

"I get it!" I said. Somebody had to stop Momo before
she fell completely to pieces over how I
might screw up school for her!

"Momo, baby," said Mom. "The wonderful thing is
that you like it here. This situation is a great
opportunity for all of us. We all want to make
the most of it— Dad, you, me, Dodo—"

"and Sven!" I said. "He is expanding his horizons, too."

"Yes," said Mom. "We all are going to just keep on
doing our best to be our best selves. And Dodo—"

"Sing something," I commanded Momo. "Sing
'River Deep and Mountain High!'" This is an old
Tina Turner song that Momo learned off Dad's iTunes.

River Deep
and Mountain
High

And the way she sings, we're all sure: she's IN.

SOME MORE THOUGHTS ON MR. DUFFY

He said that learning to keep your thoughts and questions to yourself was part of maturity and that people with self-control kept their hands still and

Dodo, hon, I don't want to set your sister up for failure. How competitive do you think things ARE in that new school?

I haven't really thought about it. There are a lot of kids, but that means there's lots to do. But, competitive...?

I think I'm going to call and ask them to let her try out for that choir.

She's sure good enough. Listen to her!

She's never had to try out for anything before. This is all new.

Everything's different now for everybody.

It's all good.

But what if Mr. Juarez is like Mr. Duffy?

It's just one class out of seven. Mr. Duffy was ALL DAY.

That's for sure. And I didn't have

DOODLING.

Mom said, "Let's leave Sven to hold the fort" and took us on a bus ride all the way here, to the Palace of Fine Arts. I think that it is the

Most gorgeous place in the city

and maybe the world!!

There is the crazy fog that comes h and the top of the bridge and Mom the Martian Singing Girl is standin on the cliff singing out to it all.

"MOM!" I yelled. "What time is it?" She showed me

"Time to be hopeful," I said

"Oh, Doodlebug Dodo, that's what I love about you," said mom.

Momo + me hanging off the bed upside down.

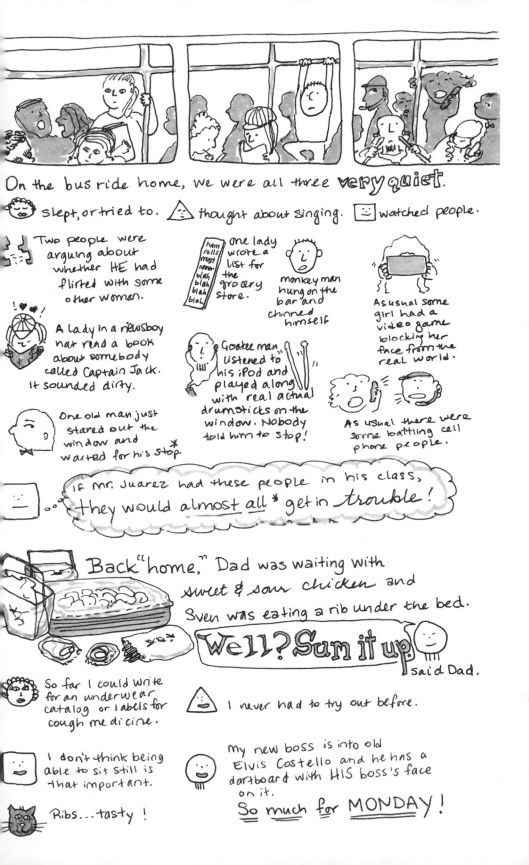

On the bus ride home, we were all three very quiet. 😴 slept, or tried to. △ thought about singing. 🙂 watched people.

Two people were arguing about whether HE had flirted with some other woman.

One lady wrote a list for the grocery store.

monkey man hung on the bar and chinned himself

As usual some girl had a video game blocking her face from the real world.

A lady in a newsboy hat read a book about somebody called Captain Jack. It sounded dirty.

Goatee man listened to his iPod and played along with real actual drumsticks on the window. Nobody told him to stop!

As usual there were some battling cell phone people.

One old man just stared out the window and waited for his stop. *

If Mr. Juarez had these people in his class, they would almost all * get in trouble!

Back "home," Dad was waiting with sweet & sour chicken and Sven was eating a rib under the bed.

Well? Sum it up. said Dad.

So far I could write for an underwear catalog or labels for cough medicine.

I never had to try out before.

I don't think being able to sit still is that important.

My new boss is into old Elvis Costello and he has a dartboard with HIS boss's face on it.
So much for MONDAY!

Ribs...tasty!

5. MR. JUAREZ

and Other Dangers

SECRET:

Even though Mr. Juarez wrote "See me" I didn't go see him. It was last period so I went and met Momo and we went home.... In the middle of the night I sleepwalked. That's what must have happened because suddenly I banged into something, and I realized I was in the kitchen at the sink in the pitch dark at 3:13 a.m., and guess what? Sven was there with me.

I GUESS I HAVE TO GO SEE HIM, SVENNY.

I believe it's best, Dodo.

I'm not telling about sleepwalking. They are all worried enough.

I think Sven has forgiven me for scaring him under the bed.

IN THE MORNING

in homeroom, I wrote this note. Cootie Catcher showed me how to fold it into an envelope. On the way to Spanish, we dropped it at the office.

Dear Mr. Juarez,
I do not doodle to be disrespectful. Doodling helps me to pay better attention. I would like to have a chance to make up the √—.
And I would like to ask permission to doodle on a separate piece of paper so it won't be on my notes.
Doreen Bussey

CLAY R US

HILL, W.   JUAREZ, M.   KELLER, D.

Mr. Juarez

"What do you think he'll say?" I worried to C.C.

"It's a reasonable request," she said.

I waited on PINS and NEEDLES until finally it was 7th period, when MR. J. Just Said NO

NO grade makeup?" "**NO** non-note doodling?" "**NO**," said MR. JUAREZ.

NO special rules for one student that don't apply to others."

"But this is **DIFFERENT**," I said. Just then I saw:

It was Momo, too upset to wait for me outside the door.

KNOCK! KNOCK!

AT FIRST, mr. Juarez was really sweet. He opened the door and asked kindly,

"Who are you?"

"**Momo!**" I said. "What happened?"

"They said **NO**!" she bawled.

"The CHOIR people? How could they?" I asked.

"I was so nervous, I could hardly sing!"

I BLEW IT! **NO!**

Maybe Mr. Juarez meant to be nice. He patted Momo's shoulder, saying,

"That's such a shame. Well, try again next year."

Maybe I should have let it alone. But instead I spoke up.

"**NO**, that's WRONG!" I said. "You should hear Momo sing!"

Mr. J said, "But the CHOIR people heard her sing."

"**NO**, she was nervous!" I said. "She never had to try out for ANYTHING before. They knew her voice in our old school and she always just got PICKED."

Mr. J said, "Was that school right about EVERYTHING?"

Momo dried her tears extremely quickly. "**NO**," she said. "They were all wrong about **Dodo**."

"It's **DOODLEBUG** now," said Mr. J. "Isn't it?"

"But not in **MATH**," I said. Mr. J. said, "Doreen,

... I took a look at your file today."

(drum roll) "Is it okay to talk in front of your sister?"

"Momo knows all about me," I said.

Mr. Juarez said, "So... borderline A.D.D.* And a somewhat optional medication that you opted out of."

I decide to open up my box of secrets a tiny inch. "I would rather handle things my own way than take stuff."

Permanent Records: PUNKS ☠

Bussey, D.

MR. JUAREZ is young for a teacher. His face is mostly nose, mustache, and eyebrows.

* Attention Deficit Disorder

FOR THE FIRST TIME, his eyes smiled. (I know that sounds weird, but.)

I'm impressed by that.

"You ARE?" I was somewhat, borderline surprised.

"Then why can't I..." "BREAK MY RULES AND DOODLE?" he asked.

"Yeah," I said. "Why?"

His eyes went all serious again. "What makes you think you need to doodle?"

I flipped my lid then. "To stop from doing all that A.D.D. stuff!!!!!!!"

(Momo held her breath.) (But Mr. Juarez did not ASK.)

He said, "There's more than one way to skin a cat."

GOOD THING SVEN WASN'T HERE TO HEAR THAT!!

"I mean," said Mr. J., "if you can do it one way, you can do it another way. Find some other ways."

Momo announced, "I am going to be in CHOIR."

Cootie Catcher was waiting in the hall.

"This is Cootie Catcher," I said. "This is Momo."

"It's really Elizabeth," she said. And Momo said,

"Miss Maureen Bussey. I'm going to sing 'O Beautiful' over the P.A. tomorrow."

"Get out, you are NOT!" said C.C.

"WAIT FOR IT!" said Miss Maureen Bussey. "And there's not going to be any choir teacher watching!"

HEAVEN HELP US oo I thought.

Momo was mad at herself, so watch out!!!

"So, did Mr. Juarez say you could doodle?" She looked like she already knew. SLY.

"No. And he meant it."

"Yup," she said cheerfully. "When Marco had him he crunched up a whole art paper Marco was working on in math."

THAT'S Wrong!

"Have you two ever been HOMESCHOOLED?" asked Cootie Catcher.

"No. Why?" "Because you think you own the world!"

HA HA HA HA HA HA HA

Momo and I laughed. "Why shouldn't we?" I said.

But Momo said, "We don't even own a CAT."

When we got home,

Dad was working late.

I was drawing CC's beautiful braids.

Momo was singing "O Beautiful."

And Mom said, "STOP EVERYTHING! I have to write about underwear."

HORRORS! TIGHTY WHITIES

WHAT? KIND? OF? UNDERWEAR? AND WHY?

"It's a tryout," said Mom.

They're from the company, they're not Dad's.

what's this hole for? Eww!

Mom has to make you want to buy them.

"Oh, no!" said Momo, then stopped herself.

"Tell me what's nice about them," said Mom. Ha Ha

"They're nice and **white**," said Momo. Ha Ha Ha

"They're SPICY and *TIGHT!* " I said. Ha Ha Ha Ha

"Okay, get out of here and let me work!" said Mom. "But first, tell me how you like your underwear to feel." We like it when she asks us this serious sort of work question.

Momo said, and I said.

1. soft
2. silky
3. short (not hanging out all over the place)
4. not pinchy

1. clean
2. cool
3. comfy (no wedgies hahaha)
4. pretty

How was your day, Svenny?

I love you, Sven.

Then we got under the bed and talked to Sven.

He didn't have anything to say in return. Momo said, "What's it like to be so scared?"

"No," I said, "how come you think you can sing on the P.A. if you were too scared in the choir room?"

"**EASY**," she said. "Nobody will be looking at me." We left Sven alone under the bed after that.

What a Wednesday!

SCHOOL OFFICE

First of all, Momo made us late. When we finally got to school, HOMEROOM had started.

Hang on a second, Dodo.

In that **second**, Momo stopped by the office. The MORNING ANNOUNCEMENTS hadn't started. I leaned close to the door and heard my sister say,

"Hi, I'm Maureen Bussey? And I was asked to sing 'O Beautiful'? At the start of announcements? Is it time now?"

And the secretary must have turned on the P. A.

O beautiful for spacious skies, for amber waves of grain...

Our little Momo sang that whole long song and she sounded like a ROCK STAR and when she was done, she said,

This has been MAUREEN BUSSEY in a song dedicated to Mr. Juarez for his inspiration.

And the school secretary said, "Thank you, Maureen. That was Lovely."

This is the COW I almost had.

HAVE YOU LOST YOUR MIND? WHY DID YOU HAVE TO DRAG MR. JUAREZ INTO IT? NOW I'M GOING TO BE IN TROUBLE AS WELL AS YOU, AND I WAS ALREADY IN TROUBLE WITH MR. JUAREZ!!

In homeroom, Ms. Keller said, "Doodlebug? Was that your sister?" YES I felt proud. "She's got the music BUG," said Cootie Catcher.

In Spanish, Señor Rámos asked, "Dorena, la cantadora, ¿es tu hermana?" "Is the singing girl your sister?" "SÍ," I said.

In Science, We talked about waves — water waves, sound waves, and music waves. I could draw.

In Social Studies, I listened to this whole big long thing about the civil war. I already had it in my old school. I doodled. And doodled. Until a hand came down on my book and Ms. Farley said, "I FIND THE DOODLING VERY DISTRACTING."

In ~~Home~~ Arts, We talked about home safety.
1. KEEP YOUR DOORS LOCKED.
2. LEAVE A NIGHT-LIGHT ON SO YOU DON'T KILL YOURSELF FALLING OVER SOMETHING IN THE DARK.
3. CHANGE BATTERIES IN SMOKE ALARMS.

At Lunch, Magic Marco asked, "Can I sit with you?" "Was that your sister on the announcements?" "What do you like best, chisel point? fine point? brush point?" all I can get! ART NERD!

In Language Arts, we are reading the worst book in the world, Lord of the Flies, and we had to talk about "Do rules matter?" "some rules hurt people", I said. Then I shut up. Why ask for trouble?

By the time I got to study hall I was half crazy. I took the lav pass and ran out, straight to Mr. Hill's room. "Can I wedge clay? PLEASE!" WHAM!

And then there was Math. Mr. Juarez watched me like a HAWK. I didn't dare to DOODLE. And at the end he said, "DOREEN?"

1. I ran upstairs to Language arts to pick up my extra assignment because I wouldn't participate in the class discussion.

2. Detention with Ms. Farley for too much doodling.

3. Marco: Hey, Doodlebug, I have something for you! (It's a folded-up paper.)
   Me: Have you seen my sister?
   Marco: Sorry...

4. I went to see if Momo was by any weird chance in the chorus room (nope: empty) on my way to helping Mr. Hill put away the clay I wedged.

5. Then it was back up to see what Mr. Juarez wants NOW!

"I know, I know," I said. "I should have stayed when you asked. But I'm already in trouble with you, so what does it matter? I had to take care of things with all my other teachers. Well, not ALL. Just some. But the other ones will probably check in tomorrow. Anyways, I have to go now and find my sister."

Mr. Juarez just looked at me funny.

As politely as I could, I said, "Mr. Juarez? What?"

He said, "You haven't seen your sister?" Then he added, "Why did she say I inspired her?" I looked at him. He really DIDN'T KNOW!

"You made her mad!" I said.

He said NOTHING. While I waited, I opened the paper Marco had given me.

"WHAT'S THAT gorgeous thing?"

It's a...

"It's very mathematical," Mr. Juarez said.

"It's just a doodle," I said. "But Magic Marco must have taken it out of the trash in Ms. Farley's room after I got in trouble for making it.

"In her class?" Mr. Juarez asked.

"Yes," I said, glaring. "And Marco 'colored' it with his Prismacolors."

"Marco Pinho?" Mr. Juarez said. "Is he a friend of yours?"

I blushed. "Can I please go home now?"

"Sure," he said. "WAIT. TAKE THIS."

He scribbled quickly on a sheet of paper and addressed it to my parents.

m/m Bussey

I left him the doodle. I read the note as I walked down the hall.

"m/m means mr. + mrs.?" was all I could say.

"I'll expect an answer tomorrow," said Mr. Juarez.

m/m Bussey —

I would like to talk to you. Please give me a call at your convenience.

555-1700 x259

RAT.

As I went home, I felt like a PSYCHO.

Q. Where was Momo? Why hadn't she waited for me?

Q. What did Mr. Juarez want to talk to m/m Bussey about? How were they going to get time to go to school to talk? It was obvious that I was just plain in trouble anyway....And maybe Momo was, too.

A. The Letter got HEAVIER as I walked, then ran, then walked. I DIDN'T KNOW if I wanted to HURRY HOME or never get home. AT LAST I did what Cootie Catcher would have done, and

I changed the shape of the PAPER (from a letter to TRASH)

meanwhile, at home...

Mom was writing STICKIES:

Don't talk to me, I have to think about UNDERWEAR.

cotton-y linen-y tight-y white-y

PANTS without RANTS — just RAVES!

marshmallows clouds teeth sheets vanilla ice cream black paper ivory light polar bear

speaking of Psychos...

protective casing for the family jewels

Stays white all night

Won't fray all day

Sticky underwear?

smooth cool refreshing

won't ride up no matter what horseback riding bicycle riding tango dancing

makes you feel like a kid again!

you won't even know they're THERE!

WHERE'S MOMO?

HERE'S MY SUGGESTION: "MOON OVER S.F.!"

6. I DON'T KNOW WHAT
TO CALL THIS CHAPTER.

Sven, Swedish kitty you should have been there wh Momo sang. She rocked the school Sven, and you'd have been proud.

Momo didn't talk to me for a long time, so I talked to Sven and listened to Mom typing. Finally, she said, "WHY DON'T YOU LEAVE SVEN ALONE?"

"BECAUSE, I like him."

"WELL, he doesn't like you!" She sat up. She had been crying....

"Mo, how come you didn't wait for me?"

"I was in DETENTION!" (WHOA! That never happened before!)

? "HOW COME?" (But I had my suspicions.)

"Ms. Wu! The PRINCIPAL! For lying to the secretary about the P.A. I hate this school!"

"I DON'T! I don't know why, but I don't!" (This was only half a lie.)

Then Mom came flying in!

"DODO! Is this your idea of HUMOR? Do you think it's funny to make fun of my w Do you think it's easy to sit here all day coming up with something that's going to make people buy ugly old boring tighty whities as if they were something NEW and EXCITING!"

"NO, Ma. Sorry, Ma."

But... ...After she went out, Momo LAUGHED. "Ma, I thought it was funny!" SILENCE

uh-

"You know what I think was **funny**?

You dedicating your song to MR. JUAREZ! And fooling the secretary! And then singing it all perfectly like you did! ALL DAY LONG, people asked if you were my SISTER! And I said, 'Yeah, she ought to be in choir!' And they said, 'SHE SURE SHOULD!'"...

...I knew I was right but something made me stop talking. Maybe it was the look on Aven's sphinxy face, but I didn't say to Momo, 'I'm sure they'll let you in the choir.' Because I sure wasn't sure. Not at all.

Well, what else was there to do? We did our homework...

Doreen Bussey
Ms. Michaels per. 5

Do Rules Matter?

In class I said some rules hurt people and I really think that's true. Okay, there are good rules like change the batteries in your smoke alarm or don't steal from people. But what about rules that give you only one chance to do something you're really good at, like my sister and singing, or rules that say you can't do something that will help you learn because teachers think if they let one kid draw then everyone will and then the whole school will be

---

There I was, cranking away, when suddenly Momo went insane.

"I CAN'T DO IT!"
"I DON'T GET IT!"
"THIS SCHOOL IS AHEAD OF US AND I DON'T UNDERSTAND!"

Homework Exercises
I. Convert to decimals.
1. $3/4 = .75$
2. $5/8 = $ _____
3. $16/17 = $ _____
4. $1/25 = $ _____
5. $3/10$

I tried showing her the math

$\frac{3}{4} = \frac{75}{100} = .75$? $4\overline{)100}^{25}$ $\begin{array}{r} 25 \\ \times 3 \\ \hline 75 \end{array}$

I tried showing her with money.

$1.00 $.75 ??

I tried showing her with pizzas. ? ?

Then we got the iPod.

track 1.   3/4 played song   .75
75   100

track 2.   5/8 played song   .625
62½   100

track 3.   16/17 played song   .94
94 100

track 4.   ¼25 played song
100
4

track 5.   3/10 played song   .30
30   1.00

HOT DIGGITY!

NOW PLAYING
2 of 15
SO NICE SO SMART
2.51   -0.22
MENU

All of a sudden, mom quit sayin' "THIS IS STUPID" and just started doing it.

Dad came in. That's how late it was!
"Sometimes you just need a VISUAL," he said.

For once I felt proud. QUICK, before he could ask us, I asked, "How was your day, Pops?"

His face changed so FAST. "Unbelievable."

Then he said, "MY BOSS got the AXE.

It was his own fault. He got caught talking to his girlfriend while throwing darts at the president of the company."

Mom was in the doorway. "Not the REAL president?"

"No, the picture on the dartboard!"

"Who caught him doing it?"

"Who ELSE?"

HA HA HA HA HA HA "THE **PRESIDENT**!"

Dad got very <u>serious</u>. "It won't be funny if I lose **my job**."

Mom got serious, too. "I'd better get down to business with this underwear ad. Could everybody please get out of here?"

ORT! ORT! ORT! ORT! ORT! ORT! ORT! ORT! ZZZ

Dad took Momo and me to the wharf where

SEA LIONS

were barking at the whole entire city, and after that, well, really, there was no place we wanted to live so much as the beautiful and amazingly great

San Francisco!!!!!

It was very late when we got home, and Mom was asleep, and the folder of her work was sitting on the kitchen table looking done. The LAST THING I was going to do was tell anyone about Mr. Juarez and his NOTE.

S P

MY DREAM ABOUT MR. DUFFY

ACTUALLY

It is a nightmare.
It is also what really did happen.
It is not only about him, but it all happened because he started it.

Mr. Duffy was once the coxswain on his college rowing team. The coxswain is a short guy who sits in the back of the boat facing front, and bosses the rowers, who row backwards so they can't see. This oar is his souvenir from the big race.

They won because he can yell so loud. But as if his voice wasn't loud ENOUGH, he will sometimes walk around with the oar and, just when you are not expecting it, he will not just walk by your desk he will suddenly WHACK it really hard with the oar.

Of course he'd never whack any of you with it!

There are always teachers who need to do this sort of thing.

Anyway, you might have a difficult boss one day. You might as well get used to dealing with all kinds of people.

MR. DUFFY HAD RULES:

1. Bottoms in chairs.
2. Mouths shut unless called upon.
3. Hands on the desk.
4. Eyes front.

I cry in my just about sleep thinking it.

Do I need to tell you I couldn't do it ??

EXCUSE ME, DOREEN?

← He said those words 100 times a day. He shook his oar at me. THEN one day when I couldn't stop asking questions about a movie, he sent me to the principal. Then the school psychologist. They got me labeled

A.D.D.

oo !

But I can SO pay attention. And I am NOT a drug dealer like the kids all said.

Some girls said he was cute. I HATED him. And I am bad at hating!

We're SO SORRY, Dodo.

The part where my parents cried is the part that always wakes me up.

They said it wasn't my fault.

BUT I'M THE ONE WHO BROKE THE RULES.

BUT OTHER PEOPLE ARE O.K. WITH RITALIN.

They said the adults in the situation were misguided, or acted too fast, or didn't act respectfully of me, including them, who should have known.

BUT WHATEVER MADE ME GIVE MY PILLS AWAY?

SHE DIDN'T JUST GIVE THEM AWAY, SHE TRIED TO SELL THEM!!

It was just so Mom and Dad would get their money back. Pills are EXPENSIVE.

ZZZZZZZZZZZZZZZZ

WHEN I WOKE UP, I FOUND MYSELF IN THE KITCHEN.

I stood there for a second thinking of where I was, and why. It helped to notice that Sven was there.

Oh Svenny! I don't WANT to be in TROUBLE!

meow!

I got the idea to do something for my family. I thought of Home Arts and the home safety tips. I didn't want to make noise, so I didn't check the smoke alarm batteries. We didn't have a night-light, so I turned on the light in the oven. And then I opened the door to check that it was locked.

No, Sven.

7. MOMO FINALLY GETS

LOST

!

I sat on the stairs of Staci's apartment and called for Sven until Dad woke up. He said, "You can't make a cat do anything —"

"Why?" I said. "Do they ha[ve] attention problems?"

"They're just independent thinkers," said Dad. He rigged up the door s[o] it stayed almost shu[t] but Sven could still get [in] if he came back.

" IF ?"

By morning, there was still no Sven.

"MOM will be here most of the day."

"most?"

Dad was grumbling: "I'VE got to go to work to see IF I'VE STILL GOT A JOB."

Mom was mumbling: "You'll be a sight tonight in your TIGHTY WHITE BRIEFS."

Momo was fumbling in her closet, digging through looking for blue clothes. "Dodo, do you have anything ROYAL BLUE? NO, that's not! Yes, that is!"

blue →
blue →
blue →

I was STUMBLING around exhausted, calling to Sven.

When we left, he still wasn't home.

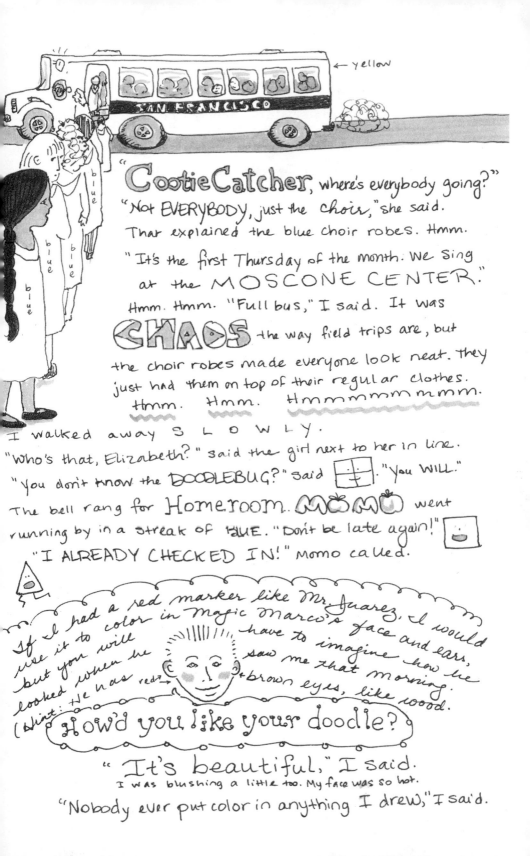

← yellow

SAN FRANCISCO

"CootieCatcher, where's everybody going?"
"Not EVERYBODY, just the choir," she said.
That explained the blue choir robes. Hmm.

"It's the first Thursday of the month. We sing
    at the MOSCONE CENTER."
Hmm. Hmm. "Full bus," I said. It was

CHAOS the way field trips are, but

the choir robes made everyone look neat. They
just had them on top of their regular clothes.
Hmm.   Hmm.   Hmmmmmmmm.

I walked away S L O W L Y.
"Who's that, Elizabeth?" said the girl next to her in line.
"You don't know the DOODLEBUG?" said ⊞. "You WILL."
The bell rang for HomeRoom. MOMO went
running by in a streak of BLUE. "Don't be late again!"
"I ALREADY CHECKED IN!" Momo called.

If I had a red marker like Mr. Juarez, I would
use it to color in Magic Marco's face and ears,
but you will have to imagine how he
looked when he saw me that morning.
(Hint: He has red + brown eyes, like wood.)

How'd you like your doodle?

"It's beautiful," I said.
I WAS blushing a little too. My face was so hot.

"Nobody ever put color in anything I drew," I said.

It was a long, nerve-wracking day.

HOMEROOM

where was Sven?

"What are the school colors?" I asked Marco.

"Royal blue and grey, like the BAY and the FOG."

"Mr. Juarez called our doodle gorgeous," I told Marco.

ESPAÑOL

Sven, come home.

Without the choir kids there, we just did book work in Spanish. I went out with the Lav Pass two times to deal with the jitters in my legs. I learned a new sentence. I didn't see Momo anywhere, but it's a big school.

SCIENCE

Svenny! Svenny!

Science! My kind of class!

We were playing with SLINKYS.

This was supposed to show how SOUND TRAVELS but I disagreed.

This isn't WORKING for me!

"EXCUSE ME, DOREEN?" asked Mr. Travis.

I said as quietly as possible:

"I think this is how one little ping might travel through the air, like the slinky moves, but not another sound."

Maybe if he had asked me to elaborate I would have clammed up like yesterday in L.A. when we were discussing Lord of the Flies.

But he gave me a box of STUFF. "SHOW ME."

And there was a jump rope in there. I laid it on the floor and pumped one end up and down and kept doing it.

"VERY INTERESTING IDEA!" said Mr. Travis.

At the end of class he said, "GOOD THINKING

In Social Studies the LAV PASS was my friend again. I can't just sit at a desk and read. Even though I was more tired than usual, I was also more nervous than usual. How could I NOT be, with Sven missing? How could I NOT be, with Dad working at a job he might lose any minute? How could I NOT be, with Mom needing so bad to get the underwear account? How?

and then there is Mrs. Juarez waiting for my parents to call and waiting for me AT THE END OF THE DAY?

was mom looking for Sven?

→ "Oh no, you don't, Miss Ants-in-the-Pants!"

"But, Miss Farley!"

"No buts!" she said, and turned away.

I got up and went to the window and looked out.

I saw MY FATHER walking into the school.

"Miss Farley! Can I go — "

"Doreen, take your seat."

I got out my pen and pad. I would quietly write her a note, explaining.

"I'LL TAKE THE WRITING IMPLEMENTS," said MS. Farley.

NO WAY! NO! NO DICE! NO! NO! NO HOW! NOT NOW NOT EVER NOT IN THIS LIFETIME! "NO!" I YELLED.

"Excuse me, Doreen?"

Every eye in the room was looking at me.

I've been trying to tell you, but you haven't been listening. My father is here! I need to tell him something about my sister.

You don't need your sketchbook for that. You're far too interested in what's going on in IT and in other parts of the school. NOW just take your seat, Doreen.

"You don't understand!" I said.

Well, PERHAPS you would like to explain AFTER SCHOOL....

I don't think anyone uses the word PERHAPS who isn't being SARCASTIC.

"No," I said. "My sister is missing and my cat is missing, so I have to go right home today. I won't have time to come see you, so can I please have my sketchbook back NOW?"

"I don't think so," Ms. Farley answered

I didn't think. I just left the room.

Trouble Time

218 down the hall

Dad?

downstairs

to the office

MS. WU pushed a new button on her phone. VERY CALMLY, VERY QUIETLY, she asked the person on the other end,

"Would you please take a look on your bus for Maureen Bussey?

Sixth grader. Brown hair. No choir robe. I'll hold the line."

"Don't worry," I said to Dad. "That's where she is."

WHY?

She wants to sing in the choir, that's all.

MS. WU said into the phone, "YOU'VE GOT HER?"

Dad made a giant SIGH. He talked into his phone.

Jolene? They found her. Guess where? She sneaked onto a school trip with the choir.... Dodo guessed it. Yup.

MS. WU asked me, "How did you guess, Doreen?"

I said, "I think she was dressed in

Camouflage

She had on royal blue, like San Francisco Bay."

"WHY?" asked Dad.

"So she could Sing, that's all," I said.

But MS. WU asked, "Why are you angry?"

said, "MY SISTER is a GOOD SINGER."

From the outer office, the secretary called,
"She's the one who hijacked the P.A. to sing 'O Beautiful'!"

"She did WHAT?" said Dad.

I said, "She deserved a SECOND CHANCE."
The secretary called, "Elspeth said she fell short
         when she agreed to give her a tryout."
I said, "She never TRIED OUT at our old school."
"And it wasn't HER fault she had to leave, it was MINE."
MS. WU asked Dad, "Are you surprised by any of this?"

"Actually, I am proud of all this."

And that is when Ms. Wu told me I could go back to
class. But not to Ms. Farley's, that was over. I made
it for the end of Shop, too late to work on anything.
There are STOOLS in shop class, same as art, and
I sat on one with my feet on the other, and stared
at my toes.

magic Marco

is in my class. He was
painting his birdhouse in
colors fit for a parrot.
"THAT'S SO PRETTY,"
I whispered.
He handed me a gold
prismacolor.

"You look like you need
some color in
your life,"
HE SAID.

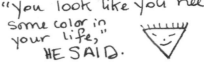

At lunch, the choir was back.

"Did I hear what? That you ran away with the choir in CAMOUFLAGE?"

"So that's what the royal blue outfit is all about?"

"You can sing, Maureen. Did they suspend you?"

"There's a meeting tomorrow with Ms. Wu and the choir teachers and me and Mom and Dad. But that's not what I wanted to tell you—"

"You think they might <u>suspend</u> you?" (To myself I said, "Or expel you?" Oh, no!!)

"Mom called!" said Momo.

"I'll bet she did!" said Cootie Catcher.

"Dodo, LISTEN," said Momo. "Mom said the lady upstairs called on Staci's house phone. They know

where Sven is!"

"WHERE⁉⁉‽"   "Up the TREE!"   "Oh, NO!"

ut Elizabeth Kaur / Colleen Callahan / Cootie Catcher said,

HE'LL COME DOWN SOONER OR LATER.
MY FATHER IS A FIREFIGHTER AND HE SAYS
THERE'S A REASON WHY YOU NEVER SEE

any CAT SKELETONS up in the TREES!

well. Thanks

Colleen!

In Language Arts, Ms. Michaels made me
read my opinion essay to the class.
When I was finished, she said,

LANGUAGE ARTS

DOREEN, AND EVERYONE ELSE,
hat do you think you should do if you
ecide a **RULE** is Wrong?"

I didn't say anything. Other people said:

SVEN IN THE TREE

O Riot!

O Rewrite the rule.

O Break the rule.

O Talk to the person who made the rule.

O Just leave.

O Quit and tell the boss why.

clipper-onner

She wrote them on the board
with a chalk pen

chalk

chalk pen body

← pusher-
upper

Imagine the
writing is white!

ms. michaels said, "DOREEN? You have a voice."
I said, "If you don't try to change things, then
NOTHING will ever change." Ouhhhhhhhhh

Chorus Time

Hang in there, Sven.

AND THEN, IT WAS CHORUS TIME.

It's just a class for singing. I don't think it's anything like CHOIR. Everybody in this school has to take chorus. I certainly don't have any "TALENT."

As I stood there singing, I thought about the rule-breaking. MOMO had broken rules just trying to get what she wanted. But wasn't what she WANTED the right thing?

AT THE END of the class I went up to Mrs. King. I noticed COOTIE CATCHER behind me trying to listen. I didn't care!

 Mrs. King, what if you tried out for choir and you didn't get in? What if OTHER STUDENTS knew you were a good singer and they got up a PETITION to get you in the choir? How many signatures would you need?

What if every signature was on an origami BIRD and we hung them all over school?

Mrs. King gave us a very fishy eye look.

You're Maureen Bussey's sister, aren't you?

YES, AND SHE SINGS LIKE TINA TURNER!

Run along, girls.

I've got a thousand paper cranes! I made them after I read this book but I had nothing to use them for! Everybody who wants Momo in the choir could sign one!

AT LAST (you guessed it)

It was period 7. Math time. Juarez time.
My sketchbook was in Ms. Farley's desk.
He wouldn't have let me *doodle* anyway.
He was going to ask me why my parents
hadn't called. He was going to keep me
after and write me another note and

I'm coming, Sven!

— — — — — — — You guessed it. I cut class. — — — — — —

I did not dare go home early. I sat next to
the mailbox on the corner and waited for
Momm. Then we walked home together.

"Oh boy, whatta day," said Momo.
"All I want to think about is Sven," I said.

Oh, thank goodness !!!

1. Mom did not say a word about school.
2. She just scooped her work folder off the table
   and headed for the door.
3. "I have to go down and present my revision," she said.
4. "I've been watching Sven since Mrs. Broccoli called
   this morning. I had just come from my FIRST
   MEETING. She said he was on the grass until he
   saw her dog, Henry. Then up he went, up the tree."
5. She pointed toward the living room window, the one
   right over our bed.

Oh, Sven! How did you get OUT THERE?

8. MOMO AND I ARE

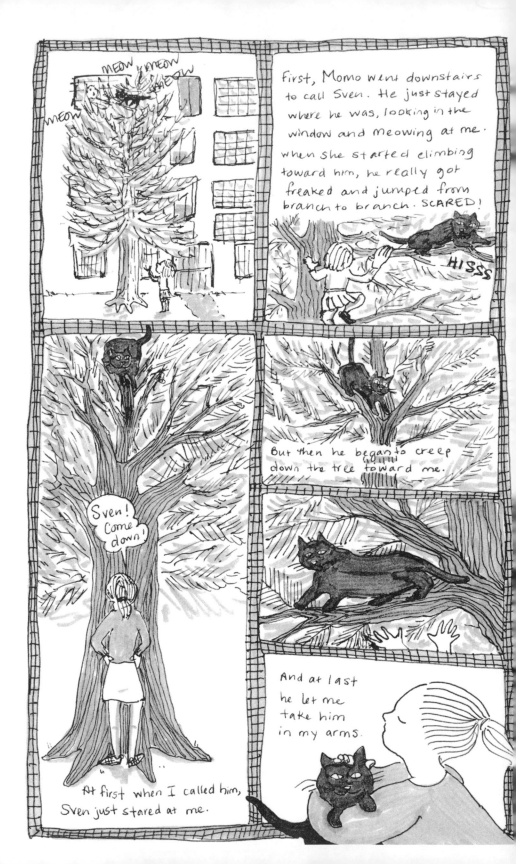

When we finally got Sven home, the phone was ringing and the message light was going cuckoo.

Ring Ring Ringy Ring Ring 4A

MOMO answered. "Hello?"

Then she said, "I'm sorry, he's not here."

And then, "No, sorry, she's not here either."

And then she said, "Um, okay, just one second."

She gave me the phone and whispered,

"MR. JUAREZ!"

Carefully, I put Sven down on the floor. He made a dash for his safe place under the bed. Back to that!

Hello?

Doreen, this is Mr. Juarez, your math teacher. ← like I forgot!

I haven't heard from your parents about that note I sent home yesterday ← we know why that is!

and I missed you in math class today ← I didn't miss you!

but I note that your parents have a meeting at school tomorrow at nine regarding your sister ← oh, really?

and so I thought I'd ask them to join me and a few other faculty ← my other teachers?

at ten o'clock in Ms. Wu's office. Have them call if there's a problem. Any questions, Doreen? ← a PROBLEM?? Yeah, there's a PROBLEM! A BIG ONE!

"No QUESTIONS!" I said.

I hung up the phone...

I said, "MO? They're meeting about you at nine?"

She only nodded. "They never met about ME before."

I said, "CONGRATULATIONS!"

She said, "They're meeting about you, too?"

(fireworks)

I said, "MOMO? We're **DOOMED**."

"...me?"

momo and I just looked at each other.

Oh, boy. We're in TROUBLE now.

mom and Dad looked at each other, then at us.

"Well," I said. "*The good news is Sven is back.*"

Then Mom asked Dad, "What meeting do YOU have?"

"The big CHEESES at work," Dad said.
"They're meeting to discuss my proposal: I told
them I wanted to take over the department."

Dad said to Mom, "I thought your meeting was today."

"It WAS," she said. "And they basically
REJECTED everything I'd worked on.
And then they picked up an idea that was
just a STICKY on the inside of my folder.
It was that underwear MOON thing of Dodo's."

"OH, NO!" I said. "Oh, Mom, I'm so SORRY!"

"Dodo, they *laughed*!" Mom said. "And they
gave me three hours to work it up. They're
meeting about my revision TOMORROW."

MOMO said,
"SO neither of you has to be AT the meetings?"

"NO," they said.

"Good," said me and Momo.

Worried

Where, oh where, is my sketchbook?

In Ms. Farley's dark desk drawer?

momo said:

"Not me. I want to be a STAR!"

What do you think will happen?

Hmm, well, were you happy with your revision?

Yes - the moon and tighty whities...

What do you think will happen?

I'm not going to get to sing with the choir that sounds so beautiful.

And Sven came out from under the bed and ate his food even though we were all sitting right there.

SVEN

I borrow a big sheet of paper from Dad to make this page. I draw + draw + ...

you just be yourselves, girls, and you will just naturally be STARS.

Well...?

Well, who would have thought they had so much in common?

Maybe you WILL...

But it's just a matter of time before all my teachers act like Ms. Farley...

Maybe they WON'T.

The stands selling strawberries on the coast road seemed a million miles away.

Dad sits with a pad making a list of...?

Jolene, what do YOU want?

I want to get the account at TW and have Dodo's and my idea all over San Francisco.

What do you think will happen?

Depends on if they think you have the experience they need.

Maybe I don't.

"ENOUGH WORRYING!" said Mom. "Who wants EGGS?"

L.A. seemed like a year ago, not a week. NO! We ALL wanted to stay right here in S.F.

Dodo, what do you want?

"I just want to be myself."

Dad said,

I think I've finally realized I want to be a big cheese.

Who would have thought I'd be this interested in the human eye?

You don't just want to draw anymore?

momo had an extra English muffin with 10 tons of jam

momo's

under the underwear moon......

Did I mention that I thought Colleen Callahan/ Cootie Catcher/ Elizabeth Karr was **TRICKY**?

Here's what she was doing when we got to school Friday morning. I don't think Momo saw what was going on. She went right to the office with Mom and Dad for her meeting about choir itself.

SIGN A CRANE! LET MAUREEN BUSSEY IN THE CHOIR!

MOMO

LET THE SINGER SING!

You took a paper crane from C.C., who had obsessively folded a thousand of them plus whatever more she did last night. Then you borrowed a PRISMACOLOR pen from Magic Marco and signed your name.

STICK THEM ON THE WALL, OR ANYWHERE!

I signed a royal blue one and taped it to my forehead and got busy tearing more tape.

Momo Elizabeth Karr

Momo Marco Pinho

Momo? Austin Mmm?o

Momo Mollie Battista

Momo Elana Killer

Momo Brian Golgas

By 9:30,

EVERYONE who was coming to school, on time, early, or late, had arrived, received a crane, and decided whether to sign it with Marco's markers, to just keep it, or to toss it, which is just a grotesque waste of paper, craftsmanship, and talent!

I finished taping cranes to Walls, Bulletin Boards, Doors, and Lights.
I made a little bow to Cootie Catcher.
I made another bow to Magic Marco.
I said, "Thank you for doing this. This might be the last time I ever see you. But I'll never forget you. You're my friends."

You're so WEIRD. That's why we like you.

Speak for yourself, Elizabeth.

Marco did not say why he liked me.
But his cheeks changed color again. — pink

They went off (late) to their classes.
I went off (early) to my doom otherwise known

MS. WU'S OFFICE

"You're not until 10, lovey, so just take a seat," said that same secretary. (Inside the office, I could hear voices: Momo, Mom and Dad, Ms. Wu, and that same choir teacher.)

I said, "I don't even know your name yet."
The secretary said, "I'm Mr. Stein."

Mr. Stein said, "Ms. Wu, I'm so sorry!"

Ms. Wu sighed. "The Bussey girls!"

I stole a glance at my sister. "Wait'll you see, Mo."

"See what?" they all said.

"They are cranes for choir," I said.

"But I'm not IN choir," said Momo, who didn't get it.

"YOU ARE NOW," said Ms. Wu, who did.

MOMO'S PEACH FACE LIT UP. "THANK YOU!" she cried.

"Don't thank ME," said Ms. Wu. "The people have spoken."

"AND YET," Ms. Wu added, "what kind of a precedent do we set if we reward illegally stowing away on trips?"

"Are you going to suspend me? Expel me?"

Ms. Wu sat down so she could look Momo in the eye. "Would I let you in choir and expel you from school?"

for two seconds, I felt better. Then Ms. Wu asked me, "Doreen, who's responsible for the choir cranes?"

I was silent.
But then I said, "NO, I won't tell you."

And Ms. Wu said, "That's what I thought you'd say."

And she *smiled*.

"Girls," she said. "I'm going to stay here for a few minutes and talk to your parents."

INSIDE MY STOMACH

Butterflies began flying.

Momo and I thought we'd just wait outside but

Ms. Wu said, "Mr. Stein? Please send the Bussey girls to bring down Elizabeth Kaur and Marco Pinho."

oh no, oh no, oh no. Ms. Wu didn't need ME to name the culprits!

What's going on?

My meeting's over! why am I still here?

Wow, thanks for the cranes!

You're an alto, right?

I wasn't even supposed to bring all the markers. My Dad...

SLOWER... SLOWER... SLOWER...

Meanwhile, back at the office, it was ten o'clock and mr. Juarez had showed up. I could hear his voice — and (oh, no!) ms. Farley's. MRs. King must have stayed. That other deep voice was MR. Hill's ... and the woman laughing? Ms. Michaels!

"NEVER!" she sang out. Then it got quiet again.

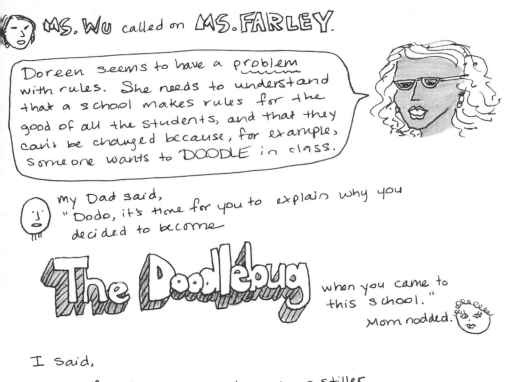

MS. WU called on MS. FARLEY.

Doreen seems to have a problem with rules. She needs to understand that a school makes rules for the good of all the students, and that they can't be changed because, for example, someone wants to DOODLE in class.

my Dad said, "Dodo, it's time for you to explain why you decided to become

The Doodlebug

when you came to this school."
Mom nodded.

I said,

"I found out it helped me keep stiller.
   I could think clearer when I was doodling.
   I didn't need to get up and go out all the time.
   I could listen and pay attention."

Ms. Farley said, "She <u>does</u> go to the lav too much."

I said, "Because you yelled at me for doodling and then took away my notebook!"

you mean old Cow!

I kept my thoughts about Ms. Farley to myself.

Ms. Keller said, "I think we know more about alternative learning styles than we are acting on."

Mr. Hill said, "I think Doreen's pretty fair at figuring out what she needs to do."

Ms. Michaels said, "Doreen could be a SHINING STAR at this school if we gave her a voice."

Ms. King said, "She certainly has made some STEADFAST friends in her first four days."

And then MR. JUAREZ spoke up.

He said, "**Doreen's** not the only **VISUAL LEARNER** in this school. She's not even the only one with an ALTERNATIVE LEARNING STYLE. But she- and her friends outside- seem *uniquely* able to figure out how to bring out the best in themselves and others. Here's a

SHOW & TELL :

what is...

What IS? this thing? OOTT-CATCHER

"Señor Ramos suggested I take a look at Doreen's 'how to' for paper folding."

"There are directions for wedging clay, too," said Mr. Hill.

("Vital skills!" muttered Ms. Farley.)

"There's a very scientific diagram of the eyeball," said MS. Wu. "Mr. Travis wrote me a note about that - and a few other demonstrations Doreen did in science."

(my eyeballs were popping at the idea of everyone checking out my sketchbook. But it seemed to be backfiring on MS. Farley, who must have offered it up.)

MS. Keller contributed, "That's a very nice picture of the school."

Ms. King pointed out the music for "O Beautiful."

"**Now for math**," said MR. JUAREZ.

MIDDLE SCHOOL

"She draws patterns," he said. →

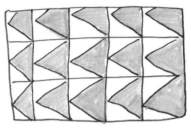

"Good grief," said Mom.

"Hoo boy," said Dad.

(They were smiling.)

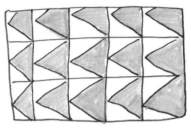

"She made a Venn diagram ← of her parents' opinions on Jr. high."

"She draws mathematical doodles, like an Altair design — and she got a friend to provide color!" →

(I blushed.)

track
1. 3|4 played song

75   .75
100

track
2. 5|8 played song

62½   .625
100

"And whoever heard of using an iPod to teach decimals?"

"I thought of it myself," I said.

"Exactly!" said Mr. J.

"I'd like Doreen — el mean, The Doodlebug — to work on the section of the school Web-site that's dedicated to homework support. And if she can prove that her doodles are helping her learn other subjects besides math, maybe we can find ways of sharing the doodles with other kids."

"SHE'LL HAVE A TOUGH JOB CONVINCING ME," said Ms. Farley.

Let me try! I said.

Then Ms. Wu opened the door and let Momo, C.C., and M.M. The teachers all filed out. Mr. Juarez squeezed my shoulder as he went by.

Then Mom and Dad got up to go. Their eyes were full of words they didn't need to say to Momo and me, because it was like we could hear them.

"**Good Luck!**" said Momo, and then I snapped to attention and said it, too.

Ms. Wu looked questions at us. "It's a big day for all of us," said Dad.

"They have **MORE** meetings," said Momo.

"WHEW!" said Ms. Wu. "Some days are like that. Just one second..." and she sat down in front of Cootie Catcher and Magic Marco in that way she had with Momo. She made them a speech

> I appreciate what you did and the civilized, peaceable, creative way you did it. You've succeeded.

And right away, Momo started singing "O Beautiful!"

COME TO CHINATOWN.

That is all Mom and Dad said to me and Momo when they came home that night. Momo and I had been wondering and worrying all day, and so, I think, had Sven. Just when he was getting *used to us*, wouldn't it just be terrible if everything for them went wrong, just when school was looking better for Momo and me?

They wouldn't answer our questions!!!

"FIRST THINGS FIRST," they kept saying all the way to town....

Finally, we got to this store Mom wanted us to look in.

"See those STAR lanterns? I want both my ☆s to choose one."

I picked a purple one. Momo's was gold. "Where are we going to put them?" Momo asked. "In the front window over your bed?" said Mom.

"But, Mom," I said. "Did you get the thing? Are we staying?"

Dad said, "Get a waving cat, too."

fish kites

fortune cookies

tangerines

It was going to be Chinese New Year soon and there were lots of good luck objects.

When we had our star lights, Dad said, "WELL. Both of our answers were very nice *maybes*. I am interim manager. Interim means 'for now.'" And Mom said, "I'm making a sample underwear ad."

"what does all this mean?"

It means, we're staying in S. F. for now.

It means, Sven is our own cat for now.

It means, Dad's job is safe for now AND
        he gets a tryout for another one.
    (And yes, Momo, he IS nervous, but hopeful.)

It means, Mom gets to try out with my idea
        for the Tighty Whitey ad, plus her words:
Reliable cool serene familiar bright

It means, for now it's a pretty happy ending
(and that's the luckiest
you can be sometimes)
and maybe, just maybe,
definitely maybe
we'll be able to stay
here for good, here
where we like our school
and our school (mostly!)
likes us, here with the
sea lions in San
Francisco, under
the underwear
moon.

The End   DB

P.S.

Naturally at school it is not all starlight and fortune cookies.

These girls came up to me in gym class and they said,

DOODLEBUG! Do you think you're so great just because you can **DRAW?**

I said,

Would it be greater if I couldn't draw?

But it made me feel very small...

But I felt a little bigger when Mr. Hill told me that by middle school most kids lose art confidence. (I am so glad ~~this~~ didn't happen to me.)

...Juarez- ow about ome artistic support for the web page?

http://www.itsdifferentfromathleticsupport.hahaha/

So, you think you're **NOT SO GREAT** because you can't draw? I have **2 WORDS** for you:

Ed Emberley

Ed Emberley's BIG ORANGE DRAWING BOOK ★★★★

and I hope nobody minds if I write him a little advertisement because anyway it's my new career besides he rocks because he will make you feel like you can draw cool things like alligators and tanks PLUS he understands how you might only have enough money for one _marker_.

He shows you how to draw things so you won't think it's all so **impossible** and maybe you will feel how I do if I sing in the shower, like maybe there's

"hope" so just don't listen to anybody who says,

Is somebody doing something to the CAT or is that you singing?

click here for help drawing cats!

I THINK drawing is in your **BRAIN** not your **Hand!**

So either PLAN your picture out of shapes like Ed E., or like Momo says this girl Lily in her class makes cats:

Meow!

cartoony
(PLAN)

or LOOK really hard at a cat and try to copy the way I did drawing Sven 800 times:

realistic
(LOOK)

If you want to know how bad my drawing from looking can be, look at my tower mistakes at the beginning in Ojai !!! Oh, the horror! But even then I was hooked! I was the Doodlebug even though I stunk because I didn't care!

Here is a partial list of things I love to draw:

seagulls

alphabets
+ shadows

ladybugs

cupcakes

fancy drinks
("Shirley Temple,"
no alcohol)

baseballs
(Go, S.F.
Giants!)

Volkswagen
Beetle

chicken
triangle

crazy guy

my name in lights!

Pencil

dead-tired
doodlebug

Try it! IGNORE MISTAKES. Doodle on, **DUDE!**

Thank you for reading this **FEIWEL** and **FRIENDS** book.

The **FRIENDS** who made Doodlebug possible are:

- Jean Feiwel, publisher
- Liz Szabla, editor-in-chief
- Rich Deas, creative director
- Elizabeth Fithian, marketing director
- Holly West, assistant to the publisher
- Dave Barrett, managing editor
- Nicole Liebowitz Moulaison, production manager
- Jessica Tedder, associate editor
- Allison Remcheck, editorial assistant
- Ksenia Winnicki, publishing associate
- Kathleen Breitenfeld, designer

Our **BOOKS** are friends for... **Life**.

Find out MORE about our authors and artists and our future publishing at www.feiwelandfriends.com